To Clair without an *e*
and home wherever that
may be —Eugenia

For 爸爸 and 媽媽. 我愛你 ❤
—Vivienne

About This Book

The illustrations for this book were sketched and colored in Photoshop. This book was edited by Alvina Ling and designed by Lynn El-Roeiy and Brenda E. Angelilli with art direction from Saho Fujii. The production was supervised by Virginia Lawther, and the production editor was Annie McDonnell. The text was set in Rotation LT Std, and the display type is hand-lettered.

This Is Not My Home

By Eugenia Yoh
and Vivienne Chang

LB

Little, Brown and Company
New York   Boston

"I have some big news,"
Lily's mama said.
        "But first you have to catch me!"

"Gotcha!" Lily cried.
"Now you have to tell me!"

Mama took a deep breath.

plop!

"We're moving to Taiwan!"

"We have to go back to take care of your Ah Ma,"
Mama explained.

"Please try to be understanding."

Lily was not understanding.

Not while packing.

Not on the airplane.

Not even when she saw Ah Ma.

"Welcome home!" Ah Ma said.

This is not my backyard barbecue.

This is not our car,

these are not my fireflies,

and this is not Jill.

This is not my farmer's market and . . .

This is not

7:00

8:00

12:00

"How was school?"
Mama asked.

"I miss home,"
Lily said in a
quiet voice.

"I'm sorry. I know this is not your home."

"But this is mine."

"And this is my food.

This is my house.

These are my people."

"And this can be *ours*."

這是我的家。

This is my home.